Postman Pat® and the Hungry Goat

D0294192

SIMON AND SCHUSTER

Postman Pat had a busy day ahead! Mrs Goggins had given him a pile of letters and three big parcels to deliver. There was a square package for PC Selby, a squashy one for the vicar, and a long flat one for Ajay. Pat struggled out of the Post Office and nearly collided with Dr Gilbertson.

Dr Gilbertson helped Pat get the parcels into his van. "Jess not with you today?" she asked.

"No, he's with Julian and Meera. They're putting up a tent in the garden."

"Ooh, camping. What fun!"

Pat's first stop was the Thompsons'. Alf was in the goat pen, feeding Rosie.
"Hello there, Pat, come right in!"

As Pat went into the pen, Rosie made a dash for it. She jumped into Pat's van, and started chewing the labels off the parcels.

"Oh dear!" worried Pat, "I hope I can remember whose parcel is whose!"

"Sorry, Pat," sighed Dorothy. "That goat eats everything!"

"Rosie, you naughty thing, come 'ere!" cried Alf, but Rosie was off down the road in a flash. "Oh 'eck! There'll be no stoppin' her now!"

"We'll catch her up in the van," suggested Pat. "I'll deliver my parcels on the way."

Julian and Meera were having a bit of trouble of their own. The tent was harder to put up than they thought, and they ended up in a big tangle!

Luckily, Jess found the sheet of instructions in the tent bag.

"Well done, Jess!" grinned Julian. "Now we can put the tent up properly!"

Reverend Timms was watering his flowers when Pat and Alf drove up.

"Hello, vicar," called Pat, "I've got a parcel for you!"

"How lovely!" smiled Reverend Timms.

"I hope it's the right parcel. Alf's goat ate the labels!" explained Pat.

"Have you seen her, vicar?" asked Alf.

"No, I've been out here all morning, looking after my . . . oh dear!"

Rosie was munching away at the vicar's flowers.

"I'm right sorry, vicar," said Alf. "We'd better catch Rosie before she eats anything else, Pat."

"Too late, Alf," said Pat, as Rosie scampered off.

PC Selby
had just
finished
hanging
out his
washing.
He didn't
see Rosie
eyeing
up his
trousers . . .

But when Pat arrived, PC Selby was very cross!

"Hello, there, Arthur, delivery for you," said Pat. "And have you seen a goat, by any chance?"

"A goat, is it? Well, if I catch that goat, it's in a lot of trouble. It's eaten my best trousers!"

"Sorry, Arthur," said Alf, "can't stop – we've got to find Rosie!"

Pat gave PC Selby the long, thin package and zoomed off down the road.

"Oi! What about my trousers?" called PC Selby.

Pat and Alf delivered the last parcel to Ajay.

"Oh good," Ajay smiled. "I've been waiting for my new 'left luggage' sign. Hmm, this feels a bit squashy to me . . . Hey! My flowers!"

Rosie was having another little snack.

"Now's our chance, Pat," shouted Alf. But Rosie scarpered before they got close.

Pat and Alf searched all over Greendale, but Rosie was nowhere to be found.

"Ooh 'eck, Pat," sighed Alf. "Where can that goat be?"

"We'll just have to keep looking, Alf. We can't give up now!"

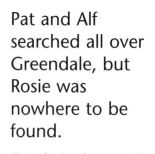

Julian and Meera hadn't given up either – the tent was finally up!

"Well done, you two," grinned Sara. "Now it's picnic time."

Julian and Meera laid the food out on a blanket but while they went to fetch the sausages and lemonade. . .

. . . the picnic vanished!

"Oh no!" wailed Julian. "Who's eaten our picnic?"

"Hmm, I've an idea who it might be," sighed Alf, as he and Pat walked over.

"We followed a trail of petals here," added Pat. "Now where is that pesky goat?"

At that very moment, Rosie popped her head out of the tent!

"Rosie!" scolded Alf.

Just then, the vicar, Ajay and PC Selby arrived, carrying their unwrapped parcels.

"My pyjamas!" smiled the vicar.

"My sign!" chuckled Ajay.

"My helmet!" muttered PC Selby, getting out his notebook.

"Sorry!" said Pat. "I must have got them muddled up when Rosie ate the labels."

"By gum, Rosie," gulped Alf. "We'd better get you back in your pen!"

"Let's take her in my van, Alf," offered Pat.

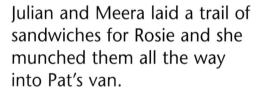

Julian and Meera laid a trail of sandwiches for Rosie and she munched them all the way into Pat's van.

"Right, Alf!" laughed Pat. "Last delivery of the day!"

They were pleased to get Rosie home.

"Thanks, Pat," said Alf.

"What a lot of trouble Rosie's caused!" said Dorothy. "We must have a picnic for everyone to say sorry."

"Grand idea!" smiled Pat.

Dorothy made a lovely picnic. She gave the vicar a new pot of flowers. "Looks like I've got a pair of trousers to mend too!" she giggled.

"Mmm, delicious cake, Dorothy," said Reverend Timms. "Perhaps Rosie should get out more often!"

"I don't think Rosie will be getting out again in a hurry," chortled Pat. "She's got a special police guard."

PC Selby stood firm by Rosie's pen. Nobody noticed as she squeezed her head through the fence and took a bite out of his new helmet!

SIMON AND SCHUSTER
First published in 2005 in Great Britain by Simon & Schuster UK Ltd
Africa House, 64-78 Kingsway
London WC2B 6AN

Postman Pat® © 2005 Woodland Animations, a division of Entertainment Rights PLC
Licensed by Entertainment Rights PLC
Original writer John Cunliffe
From the original television design by Ivor Wood
Royal Mail and Post Office imagery is used by kind permission of Royal Mail Group plc
All rights reserved

Text by Alison Ritchie © 2005 Simon & Schuster UK Ltd

A CIP catalogue record for this book is available from the British Library upon request

ISBN 0 689 87560 6

Printed in China

3 5 7 9 10 8 6 4 2